THIS BOOK BELONGS TO
A BRAVE TRAVELLER
NAMED:

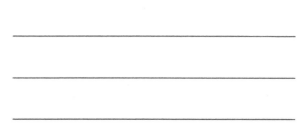

_____

_____

_____

ISBN:
978-1-961633-01-8

Visit us at auntkot.com

Tippi's First Trip

BY Aunt Kot

On a warm, breezy island, hidden in a tree,
lives a teeny-tiny creature who's hard to see.

But if you look closely, you'll spot one for sure, staring back in surprise, the wide-eyed tarsier.

Most tarsiers like to cuddle up in the trees and sleep all day among soft rustling leaves.

Nanay said, "The world is big. You are small. You're just a tarsier, two inches tall."

"You might get kicked. You might get smashed. The world's too hard, it moves too fast."

Tippi packed, then gasped, "Oh no, what now?"
when up walked a friendly carabao.

Tippi called, "How far and wide you roam.
How did you take your first trip from home?"

Moo...oove one step!

The carabao lowed, "Here's what I do. I start with one step. And you can too."

Tippi watched one step turn into two, then three, and thought, "If carabao can, then why not me?"

Up ahead, rolling hills stretched out like the sea. Tatay called, "I came to bring you back to our tree."

Tippi said, "I'll take a step, I'll find a way. I can not, will not, back away."

Tippi chirped, "How fun, a rolling hill."
Tatay barked, "Watch out, you'll take a spill."

Tatay stumbled. Down they both tumbled.
"I should've stayed at home," he grumbled.

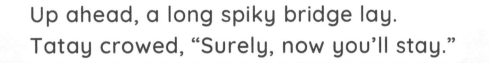

Up ahead, a long spiky bridge lay.
Tatay crowed, "Surely, now you'll stay."

Tippi said, "I'll take a step, I'll find a way.
I can not, will not, back away."

Tippi ran, so Tatay followed,
as the bridge shook, then it swallowed!

Tatay moaned, "This is a crocodile's back.
I hope he doesn't want a tarsier snack!"

Up ahead, a garden of butterflies fluttered.
"They're too bright! I can't see a thing," Tatay muttered.

Tippi said, "I'll take a step, I'll find a way.
I can not, will not, back away."

Tippi asked one, "Can you give me a lift?"
Then up high, on silky wings, they did drift.

Tippi squealed, "How lovely to travel by wing."
Tatay warned, "If we fall, it will really sting!"

Up ahead, a waterfall crashed, it thundered.
"How will you get around that?" Tatay wondered.

Tippi said, "I'll take a step, I'll find a way.
I can not, will not, back away."

Tippi cried, "No way up or down, just through."
Tippi grabbed a vine and off they flew!

Tatay complained, "We could've drowned.
Why can't you stay put on the ground?"

Up ahead, rice fields spread out like a maze. Tatay cried, "We'll be lost for days and days!"

Tippi said, "I'll take a step, I'll find a way. I can not, will not, back away."

Up ahead, Tippi heard a pounding beat,
the clip-clop of hooves and the tip-tap of feet.

Tippi said, "I'll take a step, I'll find a way.
I can not, will not, back away."

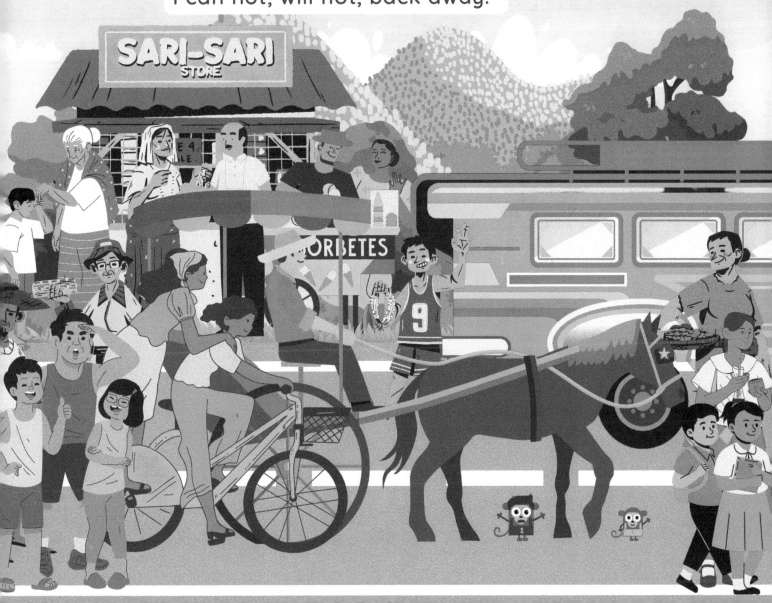

They boarded a jeep. It rocked. It sputtered.
"We're getting close. Stay strong," Tatay muttered.

The end of their trip to the trip was near.
Soon, family would be far. And Tippi felt fear.

Up ahead, at last, the airport lay.
Tippi cried, "You were right. I think I'll stay."

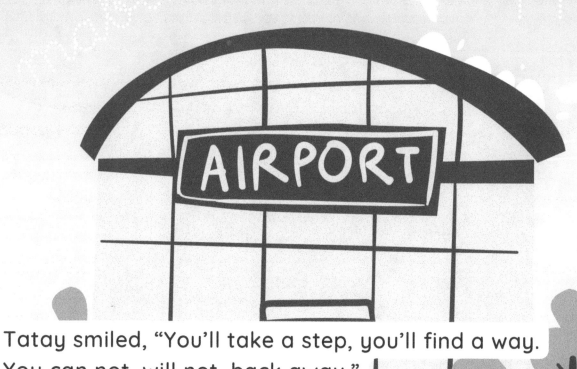

Tatay smiled, "You'll take a step, you'll find a way. You can not, will not, back away."

They marched inside, they stood in line.
Tippi hugged Tatay one more time.

BALIKBAYAN BOX

CHECK-IN

Tatay beamed with pride, "Soon the world will see how great the adventures of a tarsier can be."

Tippi buckled up. The plane soared so high.

Adventure was waiting. Tippi waved goodbye.

LEARN ABOUT THE PHILIPPINES
NEW WORDS

Dad in Tagalog

Mom in Tagalog

A small bus

Tarsier in Tagalog

The 10th largest
Philippine island

Bohol's famous
cone-shaped hills

LEARN ABOUT THE PHILIPPINES
WORD SEARCH

```
P  W  I  S  K  Q  R  R  C  T  Z  T  O  S  N
J  S  T  O  P  Z  O  M  P  A  I  V  L  N  A
O  L  E  K  K  T  U  R  Z  P  X  P  B  O  N
I  L  W  J  M  A  M  A  G  K  I  C  P  T  A
T  I  R  G  I  T  R  I  P  H  E  Y  Z  I  Y
B  H  H  O  L  A  F  Q  E  Y  I  G  S  E  L
U  E  C  A  R  Y  E  T  E  C  I  R  N  V  K
X  T  L  V  E  E  A  Y  A  A  H  P  Z  R  B
O  A  T  L  B  L  B  H  F  X  E  O  P  E  O
S  L  G  I  O  G  Y  U  O  E  Y  C  U  S  O
B  O  H  O  L  P  M  W  J  I  N  X  A  N  M
E  C  O  U  C  M  Z  J  H  M  O  T  Z  O  Q
U  O  Z  G  H  V  H  L  K  M  E  P  D  C  Y
A  H  S  V  T  W  K  M  Y  H  M  X  A  L  Z
N  C  X  E  X  A  I  C  E  P  X  Z  G  P  J
```

Tatay	Chocolate Hills	Jeepney
Nanay	Bohol	Mamag

Printed in the USA
CPSIA information can be obtained
at www.ICGtesting.com
LVHW071441290723
753672LV00006B/23